Parsifal Rides the Time Wave

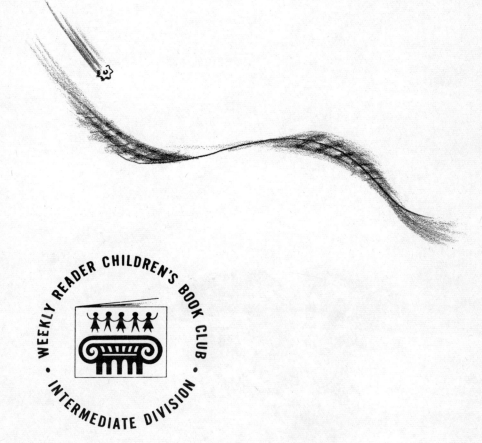

Weekly Reader Book Club

PRESENTS

Parsifal Rides

the Time Wave

Nell Chenault

Pictures by Vee Guthrie

LITTLE, BROWN AND COMPANY
Boston
Toronto

Books by Nell Chenault

PARSIFAL THE PODDLEY

PARSIFAL RIDES THE TIME WAVE

WEEKLY READER BOOK CLUB EDITION

LIBRARY OF CONGRESS CATALOG CARD NO. 62-7104

Published simultaneously in Canada
by Little, Brown & Company (Canada) Limited

PRINTED IN THE UNITED STATES OF AMERICA
BY AMERICAN BOOK—STRATFORD PRESS, INC.

To my Mother and Father

Parsifal Rides the Time Wave

*P*arsifal was in a hurry. He hated hurrying because it confused him and he was apt to make mistakes in his work, but he was on an emergency call and speed was of the utmost importance.

Parsifal was a Poddley, and in case you don't know what Poddleys are, I suppose I should explain them to you. Poddleys are little green creatures about a foot high. They have long inquisitive noses, sympathetic faces, and wonderful smiles. Their clothes are a bit startling, for they wear pith helmets and long white nightgowns but no shoes or socks at all. Each working Poddley has a star pinned on his nightgown with his own special number written on it. Parsifal's number was P654321.

1

A Poddley's job is a very interesting one indeed. It is being a friend to a lonely or unhappy child until that child's problem is solved. Then the Poddley moves on to a new case. Poddleys are also rather magical. They can appear or disappear at will, and they travel to and from jobs on the time waves that run around the world, taking them to the right place at the right time. Poddleys love their work and take great pride in a job well done.

Parsifal was no exception to this rule, and since he was unusually good at handling children, he had been promoted by the Senior Poddleys to the highly regarded Poddley Emergency Squad. The Poddleys on this special squad were always ready at a moment's notice to tackle the most difficult cases.

But to get back to Parsifal. He was on a time wave speeding towards an emergency case, and his mind was in a whirl. When he had received the call from Control Center giving him his assignment, there had been no time to find out much about the child who needed him. All Parsifal knew was that a boy named Colin MacNeill in Room 401, Memorial Hospital, Centerville, Ohio, U.S.A., needed a Poddley quickly. It wasn't much to go on.

However, his stop was approaching. As the time wave flashed by Centerville, Parsifal oozed off and found himself a window ledge of a large brick building. The February afternoon was dark and dreary, and a fitful wind was chasing bits of paper around the street below him. Parsifal checked to make sure that he was invisible, and then peered through the window of Room 401.

On the other side of the glass was a boy in a bed. He seemed to be asleep. Parsifal could not see his face, but the hand that lay on the bedclothes seemed pathetically slender and fragile.

"Tch, tch," said Parsifal.

He trickled gracefully through the window and sat down in a chair that stood in the corner of the room. "Now maybe I'll have a little time to think," he said to himself.

But just at that moment, there was a brisk rap on the door. The boy in the bed turned his head slightly, and Parsifal saw a pair of unhappy

3

brown eyes in a pale, thin face. "Come in," said the boy in a small voice.

The door opened and a crisp, pretty nurse came in. She rustled when she walked, just like tissue paper. "Hello, Colin," she said briskly, and she crossed to the bed and looked down at him with a smile.

The boy looked back at her blankly. At last he said listlessly, "Hello, Miss Gray."

"I'm sorry to hear you're still not eating, Colin," she said. "I had hoped that when I came back from my week end you would have found your appetite again."

Colin nodded. "I know," he said, "but I'm just not hungry."

"Oh dear," said Miss Gray. "If you would only eat, you would get well and could go home. Don't you want to go home?"

Colin turned his face away from her and shut his eyes tight.

Miss Gray looked exasperated. "Now listen to me, young man," she said. "All the doctors and nurses in this hospital have done their best to help you. When you came here after the acci-

4

dent, we didn't think you had much of a chance. Dr. Sawyer did a wonderful job of patching you up. You're a very lucky boy. You will be able to walk and run and play just as you used to before the accident. But you don't care. You just lie there and won't even try to eat and get strong again. It looks as if we all had worked very hard for nothing, because you won't help a bit."

The boy in the bed hunched his shoulders slightly and squeezed his eyes even more tightly together.

Miss Gray gave a long sigh. "All right, Colin," she said. "That's my lecture for today. I'm going down the hall to another patient. Will you at least try to sleep a little now? That would help some."

And she turned and walked to the door. Somehow she didn't rustle quite as much. "Good-by for now," she said. "I'll see you later."

There was no response from the bed, but as she closed the door softly, she heard a muffled "Good-by." A faint smile crossed her lips as she started down the hall.

Back in Room 401, Colin began to lose himself

6

in a world that the grownups didn't know about, a make-believe world in which he and his dog Lad played together in dark forests and green meadows. They had ever so many adventures, all happy ones. Lad wasn't stiff any more and there were no gray hairs on his muzzle. Colin was just beginning a new adventure when—

"Ahem," said a small dry voice.

The make-believe world disappeared. Colin was back in Room 401. What did they want now? Why did they have to bother him so? He lay quietly, pretending to be asleep.

"Mr. MacNeill," persisted the voice.

Colin was startled. No one called him Mr. MacNeill—no one that he knew, at least. He opened one eye cautiously, but he couldn't see anyone.

"Who are you?" he asked nervously.

"I'm Parsifal, sir, your Poddley," replied the voice.

Colin sat up slowly. He was very weak and sitting up was a big effort for him. He looked around the room carefully, but he still could see no one.

"Where are you?" he whispered fearfully.

"Right here at the foot of your bed," said the voice.

Colin stared and stared, but there was nothing at the foot of his bed—nothing that *he* could see, anyway. There was a short moment of silence, and then he heard the voice say in

8

a flustered undertone, "Oh, bother! I forgot."

Almost at once, as Colin looked on in fascination, something appeared at the foot of his bed. The something was a little green man wearing a long white nightgown with a star pinned on it and a pith helmet that looked rather too big for him.

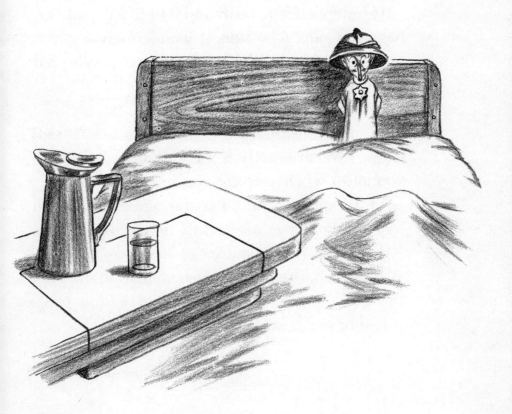

"I beg your pardon, sir," he said, "but I came in such a hurry that I suppose my wits haven't caught up with me yet. I'm afraid I must have given you quite a turn."

Colin nodded slightly, his eyes glued on the little man. "Are you real?" he asked at last. "Or are you something that I see because of the accident?"

"Oh, I'm quite real," said Parsifal cheerfully. "Here, take my hand and see for yourself."

He stepped forward and stretched out his hand to Colin, who took it wonderingly.

"You feel real," the boy admitted. "Who did you say you were?"

"Parsifal, sir, your Poddley."

"I never heard of a Poddley before," said Colin. "What exactly is a Poddley, and what do you mean when you say you're *my* Poddley?"

"I'll explain," said Parsifal agreeably. "You see, we Poddleys are mildly magical creatures whose job it is to take care of unhappy children. We love children very much and want to help them all we can, so when a child wishes for a friend or needs help, we are sent to him."

Colin scowled. "I didn't wish for anything," he said. "The only thing I want is to be left alone."

Parsifal was unperturbed. "I know," he said pleasantly. "But sometimes we find that those are the times when we Poddleys are really needed most. But now that I have explained about me, I would like very much to hear about you. We are briefed on our regular assignments but not on emergency ones, since there's so little time to spare. As you are an emergency case, would you mind telling me your problem yourself so I can begin to help you?"

Colin shook his head stubbornly. "I haven't got a problem," he said. "I just want to be left alone."

"I know," agreed Parsifal. "So you said before. But why? There must be a reason. Nobody wants to be left alone all the time."

"I haven't got a reason," said Colin flatly. And he lay back in bed and closed his eyes firmly.

"Oh, that's not fair!" protested Parsifal. "I told *you* about *me*, and I went to all sorts of trouble to come here. I think you could at least

11

tell me something about yourself. All I know is your name. How old are you?"

"Ten," said Colin. He forgot that he had made up his mind not to talk.

"Have you any brothers or sisters?" asked the Poddley.

"Nope," said Colin.

"Do you like school?"

"It's all right, I guess."

"Why are you here in the hospital?"

No answer. Colin clamped his mouth shut and turned his face away from Parsifal.

The Poddley pattered to the other side of the bed.

"Mr. MacNeill," he said firmly, "I want you to open your eyes and look at me and tell me why you are in this hospital."

Colin opened his eyes. He didn't mean to, but somehow they seemed to open all by themselves. He looked at Parsifal's pleasant face curiously. "Did you open my eyes for me?" he asked.

"Well, sort of," admitted the Poddley. "I told you that Poddleys are magical."

Colin's face lit up suddenly. "How magical?"

he breathed. "Could you bring back something that was gone?"

Parsifal looked at Colin sharply. "That would depend," he said, "on what was gone, and how, and whether it was a good idea to bring it back in the first place."

Colin sat up in bed, his eyes glowing. "I'll tell you all about me, Parsifal," he said eagerly, "if you'll promise to bring Lad back."

Parsifal smiled. "Mr. MacNeill," he said, "I never make a promise I can't keep, and I might not be able to keep that one. I will promise you one thing though—that I will do everything in my power to help you. Now suppose you tell me about yourself and this 'Lad' you care so much about."

"All right," said Colin. "I will. Because you promised to help me and the only way to do that is to bring Lad back. Lad is my dog"—he stopped and corrected himself—"was my dog." Two big tears began to roll slowly down his cheeks. "He's been my dog ever since I can remember. Mother and Dad got him when he was a little puppy, right after they had me, so we

13

could grow up together. And we did. He was a collie, the most wonderful collie in the world. Lad was my very best friend. He followed me wherever I went. He sort of looked out for me — you know. In the last year or two, though, he began to walk kind of stiffly. And he got real gray around his muzzle. Dad said it was because he was getting old.

"So I began to look out for him because he needed it, just the way I'd needed it when I was little. I didn't let him play too long, and things like that, because I thought it might hurt his poor stiff legs. I got so I'd stay pretty close to home. In the afternoons the gang would come to my house after school. They all understood about Lad and they loved him too. That worked out just fine, and Lad didn't get tired at all, because he could lie on the front porch and still see me and know I was around. And then —" Colin swallowed and stopped.

"Go on, sir," said Parsifal gently.

Colin took a deep breath and began again. He was talking very quickly now, trying not to think about what he was saying. "We were playing

15

football one afternoon," he said. "Bobby — that's one of the guys in the gang — threw a pass to me that was too high. The ball went over my head and out into the street. I went after it. I thought

I looked both ways, honest I did, but all of a
sudden there was this big truck coming at me
fast as anything. I couldn't move. Somehow my
legs just wouldn't work. And then I saw Lad

coming out of nowhere. He and the truck hit me almost at the same time. Only he hit me first. They told me later that he saved my life, because he knocked me aside so that the truck only hit me with its fender. I guess I fell and cracked my head against the curb, because I don't remember what happened then. Anyway, I ended up here with busted ribs and a bump on my head and something they call internal injuries. But Lad ended up dead." Colin began to sob. "I wish Lad hadn't saved my life," he choked, "because I don't want to be alive if Lad isn't."

Parsifal looked at the boy with sympathy. "I see," he said. "I'm very glad to know the whole story. Now maybe I can find a way to help you."

Colin stopped crying and said angrily, "But you don't know it all yet. You don't know that everybody tried to keep me from knowing that Lad was dead. If I hadn't heard Dad talking to Dr. Sawyer outside my door the other day, I wouldn't have known it yet, I guess. Dad was asking Dr. Sawyer when they should tell me about Lad, and the doctor said not to tell me until I was stronger because it would hurt me so

18

much. He was right. It did hurt me. It hurt something awful. Nobody can fix it. And they can take their stupid new puppy and go jump in the lake!" he added savagely, kicking at the sheet.

Parsifal pricked up his ears. "New puppy?" he inquired. "What new puppy is that?"

"Oh, after I told them that I knew about Lad, they got a puppy for me to take his place. They wanted to bring it over to the hospital, but I won't see it. Nothing can ever take Lad's place."

Parsifal sat down on the edge of the bed. He looked very solemn. "Mr. MacNeill," he said at last, "I know how badly you must feel. To lose something one loves as much as you loved Lad is very hard indeed. But think about Lad for a minute. Do you think he would want you to grieve this way? After all, he gave you a present. Your life. I think his feelings would be terribly hurt if he thought you didn't value his present."

Colin's eyes opened wide, and he said in a startled voice, "I hadn't thought of it like that, but I suppose you're right. I guess I should show Lad how grateful I am by getting well and going home. But, Parsifal, it will be so hard.

19

I've gotten so I'm really and truly not hungry."

"Well, let's tackle that problem right now," suggested Parsifal. "Can't you think of anything you'd like to eat?"

Colin thought hard. "I can think of something I'd kind of like," he ventured, "only I don't think they'd have it in a hospital."

"What is it?" asked the Poddley.

"A cheeseburger," said Colin with a tiny smile. "A cheeseburger with onion and lots of ketchup."

"That doesn't sound like hospital fare, I'll admit," said Parsifal. "However, I will see what I can do. I am very anxious for you to begin to get strong, Mr. MacNeill, because you must be a great deal stronger before I can give you a rather special present."

"What present?" asked Colin eagerly.

"I just thought of it a few minutes ago," said Parsifal a little smugly. "And since it's to be a surprise present in return for your getting well, I can't tell you now."

"Oh," breathed Colin, "a surprise! Parsifal, are you going to give Lad back to me somehow?"

"Not exactly," said the Poddley. And he would say no more. Instead he changed the subject. "What time do they bring your dinner?" he asked.

Colin glanced at the clock. "Gee, any minute now. I didn't realize what time it was."

"Then I had better disappear," said Parsifal.

"Why?" asked Colin.

"Because that's one of the rules," said Parsifal. "I am your Poddley and only you must see me." And, as he spoke, he vanished.

Colin blinked several times and rubbed his eyes, but the Poddley was gone. He suddenly grew frightened. Had it all been a dream? "Oh dear," he said, distressed, "maybe he wasn't real after all."

"Yes, I'm quite real, sir," said Parsifal's voice from the visitor's chair. "I'm right here, even though you can't see me, and I'm going to sit here and watch you eat your cheeseburger."

Colin laughed delightedly. "I'm so glad," he said. "And you won't leave me, even at night when I'm asleep?"

"No," said Parsifal reassuringly, "not even then."

There was a sound at the door. The knob turned and Miss Gray came in, carrying a tray. She had a big smile on her face. "Colin," she said, "I had the most wonderful idea a few minutes ago. I have a little brother who is just about your age, and I suddenly thought 'What does Jimmy like to eat?' Then I remembered, and I went to the dietician and asked her if it would be all right to give you that for supper. She said I might as well try it, because you certainly

22

wouldn't eat anything else. So guess what I've brought you!"

Colin's eyes grew bright. "A cheeseburger with onion and lots of ketchup!" he exclaimed.

Miss Gray stared at him in amazement. "How did you know?" she gasped.

Colin grinned. "I just knew," he said. "And do you know what else, Miss Gray?"

"What?" asked Miss Gray a little weakly.

"I'm going to eat it," said Colin simply. And he did.

Later that evening after Colin had gone to sleep, Parsifal looked at the clock on the wall. It was ten o'clock. "Time to call in," he murmured.

Part of every working Poddley's job is to call Control Center once a day with all the information he has about his case and how it is going. So now Parsifal proceeded to call in with his first report on the MacNeill case. He pressed his hand to the star that was pinned on his nightgown. Presently it grew warm and began to hum softly. When Parsifal heard the hum, he said in his best silent voice, "This is P654321 calling. *Repeat —* P654321 calling. Do you read me? *Over.*"

A crackling voice answered, "Control Center to P654321. Control Center to P654321. I read you loud and clear. Go ahead, please. *Over.*"

"I'm on the MacNeill case," said Parsifal. "It looked like a tough nut at first, but I think I've got it under control for the moment. Any special instructions? *Over.*"

"Good work, P654321," replied the tiny voice. "No special instructions. We'll stick with you." The voice became less impersonal for a moment. "Any mistakes?" it asked. It held a hint of laughter.

"Oh really!" said Parsifal, annoyed. "Well, all right. If you must know, I arrived here in such a rush that I forgot I was invisible and scared my employer a little. That's my only mistake so far." He was about to say *"Over and out"* because he thought he could hear Control Center laughing, but he suddenly thought of something. "Do a little research for me, will you?" he said. "Find out an exciting time in the history of the Mac-Neill family, please. It would have been in Scot-

land, I think, quite far back. I have something
definite in mind. *Over.*"

"Scotland. MacNeills. *Roger,*" said Control
Center. "I'll have it for you tomorrow. *Over.*"

"Thanks," said Parsifal. *"Over and out."*

The humming stopped and the star grew cold.
Parsifal settled back in his chair, a trifle ruffled.

He knew that even though he was highly regarded among the group in Control Center he was also a never-ending source of amusement to them. This was because he was quite absent-minded and seldom failed to make a mistake or two on a case. To the older Poddleys in Control Center who would much rather have been out on jobs, these mistakes made their work lighter and less boring. They were awaited eagerly and they relayed back and forth around the Center —"Parsifal did it again! Wait until you hear this one!"

This irritated Parsifal a bit, and now he said to himself as he settled down for the night, "I'll show them! I'll do a superlative job and then they'll stop this silly giggling for good!"

The next few days were hard ones for Colin. It was really very difficult for him to eat. He did the best he could, however, and soon he began to notice a difference in the way he felt. Mr. and Mrs. MacNeill were thrilled with the change in their son. He seemed like the old Colin again, and so his father, encouraged by his cheerful-

27

ness, mentioned the new puppy. "I know some-
one that will be glad to see you when you get
home, son," he said. "That puppy really needs
a playmate."

Colin turned his face away, and although his
mother changed the subject quickly, the visit
was ruined.

When his parents had gone, Colin looked at
Parsifal rather defiantly. "I know you think I
was rude to them," he said. "But I just can't
stand it when they start talking about that darn
puppy." He banged his fist on the bed in exas-
peration.

Parsifal gazed mildly at the angry boy. "You
seem a great deal stronger, Mr. MacNeill," he
observed. "That was quite a blow you gave the
bed just now. Does it make you feel any better?"

Colin colored slightly. "I guess not," he admitted. "I'm sorry, Parsifal. I suppose I'm be-
having badly. I don't know what's wrong with
me."

Parsifal's eyes twinkled as he said, "I believe I
have something here that might help. It's a book
which I think you will find rather interesting."

He handed Colin a small, worn volume and, as Colin studied it curiously, he added, "I hope you will enjoy it, Mr. MacNeill. Because if you do, I believe that by the time you finish it, you will be well enough to have the present I told you about the first night we met."

"What's the book about, Parsifal?" asked Colin. "Does it have something to do with the present?"

"Yes, sir, it has," replied the Poddley. "It's a history book—the story of Robert the Bruce."

Colin looked at him in dismay. "A history book?" he faltered. "Good grief, Parsifal. I hate history!"

Parsifal took this statement very calmly. "What a pity," he remarked. "Why?"

Colin frowned. "Oh, I don't know," he said. "I guess it's because it's so dull. All that stuff that happened so long ago isn't important to me. But you said this book has something to do with my present. How could it?"

"I can't tell you that just yet, Mr. MacNeill," said Parsifal. "But I am terribly sorry to hear

that history bores you so. Perhaps you don't study it properly."

"Maybe I don't," said Colin. "I read it, and then I memorize dates and names for tests. Is that wrong?"

Parsifal smiled. "Well, that depends," he said, "on what you hope to accomplish. If all you want to do is pass your tests, I suppose it isn't. However, I can see why it's boring. But if you want to *enjoy* what you're learning as well, it most certainly is wrong."

"Okay then," said Colin. "What should I do?"

"Well," said Parsifal, "the important thing is to think of these names you memorize as people —real people who think and feel just like the people you know. History is the story of people, and it is the most exciting story in the world. Everything that you know and are today is a result of the people who have gone before you, and history tells you about the most important of those people. Do you see?"

"I suppose so," said Colin.

"Well, then, let's start with the book I gave you. Have you ever heard of Robert the Bruce?"

"He was Scotch, wasn't he?" said Colin. "Oh, yes — wait a minute, Parsifal, don't tell me — he was the King of Scotland, and the English tried to conquer him, but he beat them in the Battle of Bannockburn. Is that right?"

Parsifal nodded. "That's pretty good, sir. But perhaps I can add a little more so you will know what to expect when you read the book. First of all, do you know when he lived?"

Colin frowned. "I've forgotten," he said at last.

"Well, he lived over six hundred years ago," said Parsifal, "in what you might call the Age of Chivalry. He was a very unusual man, Mr. Mac-Neill. I suppose he was the greatest king Scotland ever had. He also had some important qualities that you would do well to encourage in yourself."

"Which ones?" demanded Colin, beginning to be interested.

"Patience, for instance, and courage. And hope in the face of adversity. You see, the war that ended at Bannockburn began many years before that battle. In the beginning Bruce was

33

defeated time and time again. But he didn't give up. Instead he roamed the wilds and highlands of his country, seeking men to help him in his fight for Scotland's freedom."

"You mean he didn't have enough people to fight the English?" asked Colin. "I thought that everybody pitched in."

"Heavens no, Mr. MacNeill. Not at first," replied Parsifal. "In those days most of the Scots were scared of the English and didn't think much of the Bruce's chances. They were afraid that if they sided with him and he was defeated they would be punished by the English."

"Well, I think they were cowards!" declared Colin angrily.

"No, not really," said the Poddley. "They had their families to think of. But there were some who braved all danger to follow their King— Lord Douglas, sometimes called the Black Douglas, and of course Edward Bruce, the King's brother, and Kirkpatrick, and Lindsay, and MacDonald, Lord of the Isles, and William, Earl of Ross, and other brave men, who with their clans behind them stood firm at Bruce's side. And then, sir, there were the MacNeills."

"MacNeills!" gasped Colin. "You mean Mac-Neills like me?"

"Yes indeed," replied Parsifal. "As a matter of fact, you are descended from them. One of them, Neil Og—which means Neil the Young in Gaelic—was given lands in Kintyre by Bruce, as reward for his good services. So, you see, sometimes history can be quite interesting."

"Gosh, it sure can!" breathed Colin. "Does the book tell all about those people?"

"Yes, sir," replied the Poddley. "And a great deal more that I couldn't begin to remember."

"I think I'll start it right now," said Colin. He opened the little volume and was soon lost in the story it told. Parsifal said nothing, but watched the boy with a gleam of satisfaction in his eyes.

It took Colin three days to read the book. He read it very carefully, because he found himself fascinated by the great King and his many adventures. On the afternoon of the last day, Mr. MacNeill told him happily, "Colin, Dr. Sawyer says you can come home tomorrow!"

Colin stared at his father. He looked almost frightened, but he managed to stammer, "G-gee, that's s-swell." But his parents didn't seem to notice his confusion.

When they had gone, Colin turned to Parsifal and said, "I'm afraid to go home, Parsifal. It's all going to seem so strange without Lad."

"I know, sir," said Parsifal. "But don't worry. You'll get over that feeling very quickly. And anyway you won't have much time to think about it."

"Why?" asked Colin.

"Because I'm going to give you your present tonight, Mr. MacNeill," replied the Poddley.

"Oh!" exclaimed Colin, his face alight. "Please tell me what it is!" he begged the Poddley.

"If I did, it wouldn't be a surprise," said Parsifal firmly.

"Then I guess I'll have to try to be patient," sighed Colin. "I'll try to be like the Bruce when he was in the Highlands. You know, Parsifal," he added dreamily, "I wish I could have been there. It all seems so real to me if I think about

37

it carefully. I like to figure out how the people felt and thought—even what they said to each other. When I do that, it's almost as if they were alive."

"You will make an excellent history scholar after all, Mr. MacNeill," said Parsifal in a satisfied tone, "now that you have learned the correct method of studying the subject."

The rest of the day seemed almost endless to Colin, but it was over at last. When Miss Gray had turned out the light and he heard her footsteps go off down the hall, he whispered, "Can I have my surprise present now, Parsifal?"

"Yes," replied the Poddley, appearing suddenly beside the bed. "Yes, I think it's just about time. Do you still wish you could have been with Bruce in the Highlands?"

"Well, yes," said Colin, puzzled.

"Then, Mr. MacNeill, I'm going to take you there!" said Parsifal.

"Oh Parsifal!" gasped Colin. "But how?"

"We'll use a time wave," explained the Poddley. "Time waves are a most convenient mode of transportation. They not only take you to the

right place, like trains and buses and planes —
they also take you to the right time. Now, are
you ready to go, sir?"

"Yes," said Colin. "I mean No. What am I
going to wear? I can't go in my pajamas, can I?"

"A mere trifle," said Parsifal airily. "I believe
you will find that detail attended to on your ar-
rival in Scotland. Now, sir, we really must get
down to business or we'll miss our time wave.
Please take my hand and concentrate very hard
on nothing. Don't let one single thought creep
into your head. Keep your mind a blank."

Colin did as he was told.

"Oh, very good, sir," said the Poddley's voice.
"That's an excellent nothing!"

And then Colin had a very strange feeling. He lost all sense of weight and seemed to be floating very gently through the air. When he listened carefully, it seemed that he could hear faint music and the babbling sound of many voices. It was a very interesting feeling, indeed, but it was over very quickly. Suddenly solid ground was under his feet once again, and when he looked about him, he saw that he was in a little glen surrounded by dark trees and that the babbling sound he had heard had turned itself into the sound of the stream that ran through the glen, splashing its stones in its hurry to be off and away down the steep hillside.

Colin rubbed his eyes in astonishment. "Parsifal!" he cried. "We're really here, aren't we?"

"Yes, sir," replied the Poddley's voice from across the glen. "How do you like your new clothes?"

Colin looked down at himself and gasped. Gone were the striped pajamas he had been wearing only a moment ago. In their place he found a rough tunic belted by a narrow strap of leather and over his shoulder a heavy tartan in the muted colors of the MacNeills. Hanging from his belt was a sheathed knife, which he later learned was called a dirk. His head was bare and on his feet were curious shoes, which seemed to be made of untanned hide.

"Parsifal, where are you?" he called. "Come look at me, quick!"

"Here I am, Mr. MacNeill," said Parsifal, appearing at his side. "Well, you look the proper Scotsman, if I do say so myself," he added as he surveyed his handiwork.

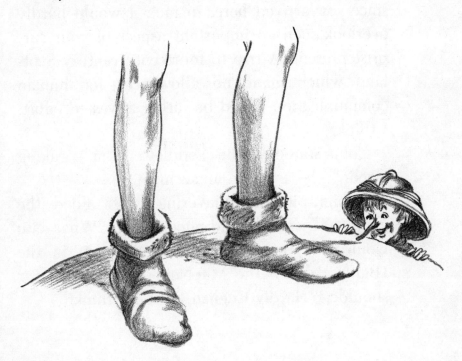

"It's just wonderful!" breathed Colin. Suddenly he looked at the Poddley in dismay. "Parsifal," he groaned, "do you realize that I won't be able to understand anybody and they won't be able to understand me? The book said that they all spoke Gaelic, except for a few who could speak French. I'm not very good at French, and I don't speak a word of Gaelic!"

Parsifal smiled quietly. "You don't realize it, Mr. MacNeill, but you have been speaking excellent Gaelic for about three minutes — ever since you arrived here, in fact. I would hardly overlook such an important aspect of your surprise present. A trip to fourteenth-century Scotland which made no allowances for human communication would be rather a wasted effort, I think."

Colin stared at the Poddley. "I'm speaking Gaelic?" he asked in amazement.

A high-pitched, quavering laugh filled the glen, and a voice said mockingly, "What else would you be speaking, lad, and you in the Highlands with the MacNeill tartan over your shoulder? Hardly English, I would think!"

Colin jumped. He looked around the clearing and suddenly saw an old man standing by a rock, leaning on a twisted staff. His raiment was dust-stained and travel-worn, but his eyes were merry as he stared back at the bewildered boy.

"Good morrow, Colin MacNeill," he said. "May I be the first to welcome you to our fair country? You wear an honorable plaid, and I have no doubt that you will add to its glory before the day is through. Come now, friend Parsifal," he added, "don't try to play me for the fool. Your little tricks may suffice for ordinary mortals, but you forget that *I* am a somewhat different kettle of fish."

Parsifal, who had disappeared when the old man first laughed, appeared again immediately and said dejectedly, "Confound it all, Tamas. It's really very discouraging. I thought that I had learned the art of vanishing rather well."

"Oh, make no mistake, you vanish very well indeed," returned the old man, his eyes twinkling more merrily than ever. "But surely, Parsifal, you cannot expect to bewilder Tamas of Ercildoune with your magic. To one who has been

given the gift of second sight, this poor world, and even what's beyond it, holds no mysteries."

Colin gazed at the ancient stranger with growing wonder. "Are you really the Wizard of Ercildoune?" he breathed. "The one who was called Tamas the Rhymer?"

Tamas glanced at the boy in some amusement. "Aye, I am he," he replied. "I see my name is known in tomorrow's world then. What do you know of me, Colin?"

"Well, that you were kind of a legend in Scotland and that you visited in Fairyland with the Queen of the Fairies and when you came back you could tell the future and things like that. I didn't quite believe it all," Colin added thoughtfully. "The part about Fairyland, I mean."

Tamas's face grew solemn as he said, "And you would not be the first to disbelieve, nor the last. But let's talk of other things. You've no time to waste prattling of Fairyland, you know. You've come to see the Bruce and to help him."

Colin nodded vigorously.

"Well, you can soon be of help," said Tamas. "He's hunting alone not far from here, but he's

45

in great danger. There are three traitors searching for him — a cousin of the King's and two of
his sons. They mean to kill him. If you are quick
you can warn him."

"How can I find him?" cried Colin.

"Follow the burn," replied the old man. "You
will find him resting beside its banks. Farewell,
Colin MacNeill, and Godspeed!"

As he spoke, his shape grew dim before Colin's
startled eyes, until it was gone entirely and all
that was left was a slight mist, that swirled for
a moment over the greensward and then faded
away altogether.

"Parsifal," gasped Colin, "where did he go?"

"I think perhaps to where his heart has been
for many a year," answered the Poddley softly.
"But now, sir, let us make good use of his knowl-
edge and find the Bruce. I'm going to disappear.
But don't worry, I'll be with you at all times."

"All right, let's go!" said Colin, and he turned
and pelted off down the steep hill, following the
path of the rushing stream. It was a twisting,
difficult path. Colin had to clamber over great
boulders and leap small gullies that opened be-

46

neath his feet. Once he paused to catch his breath, but he heard Parsifal's voice close beside him. "You can't stop now, Mr. MacNeill," it said. "There is no time to be lost."

So on he went. His heart was beating wildly, and his lungs seemed ready to burst, but suddenly he came into a clearing and saw a man sitting beside the stream. A bow lay near him on the grass, and a dog was at his side. The dog raised its head and barked at Colin, and then the man looked up. When he saw the boy he smiled, and Colin fell on one knee before him. Even if he had not been told, Colin would have known that this was the King. There was nothing in his apparel to suggest royalty, but something in his face and manner proclaimed his heritage. His eyes were kind as he looked at the boy, and his voice soft when he said, "You seem to have come a long way at a fast pace, lad. Sit down and rest a bit with me."

"Sire!" gasped Colin. "You're in great danger. Your cousin and two of his sons have turned traitor to your cause and are on their way here to kill you! I came to warn you."

The King looked sharply at the boy and said, "You're a MacNeill, I take it, from what you wear on your shoulder. How did you know of this plot?"

"From Tamas of Ercildoune, sire. I met him on the mountain, and he told me where to find you."

Bruce seized his bow and stood up. Colin saw that besides the bow he was armed with a short sword. "I had not thought the Rhymer was still with us," he mused. "He has not been seen now for many a year. But he was ever a man for freedom. Perhaps he came once more to help the cause of Scotland."

Turning to Colin, he said, "What is your name, lad?"

"Colin MacNeill, sire," replied Colin. "And, oh, please, can't I help you fight them?"

The Bruce looked down at him gravely. "No, Colin," he said. "You will be more valuable to me in another way. Take Bàn with you"—he motioned toward the dog—"and stand at the edge of the glen where you can see but cannot be seen. Then if all does not go well—if I should

49

be wounded or killed—you can find my Lord Douglas and tell him what has passed. He is camped about four leagues from here. You have only to follow the burn to find him. Now go and hide yourself. And, Colin," he added, as the boy started for the trees, "accept the heartfelt thanks of the King of Scotland. I hope that before this day is out I can show you the full measure of my gratitude."

"It is enough to help you, my lord," Colin faltered. "I ask no more than that."

He reached the edge of the glen and whistled to the dog, which stood silent and still by the stream, watching his master. When he heard the boy's whistle, he looked towards him and then back to Bruce questioningly. "Go, Bàn," said the King. He lifted his bow and pointed to Colin. "Go with him and obey him."

The dog dropped his head and tail dejectedly and walked slowly to Colin, who looked at him sympathetically. "Come here, boy," he said. "I know how you feel. Lad used to look the way you do when I couldn't take him with me and had to leave him behind."

51

Bàn looked into Colin's face, and Colin realized with a shock that the dog looked like Lad. He was a collie of sorts, which may have accounted for part of the resemblance, but it was something in his eyes and expression that reminded Colin so much of Lad. Bàn seemed to have the same feeling of recognition, for he gave a little sigh and lay down quietly at Colin's feet. Colin knelt beside him and stroked him gently. "Parsifal," whispered Colin, "are you there?"

"Yes, sir," replied the Poddley. "I'm right here."

"Parsifal, Bàn is so much like Lad," said Colin wonderingly. "He doesn't have the same color or shape really, but he looks like him just the same."

"I never saw Lad," said Parsifal, "so I can't compare their outward appearance, but from what you have told me about your dog, and from what I know of Bàn, I think that you are right. Inside they are very much alike."

Just then there was a sound to Colin's left. He crouched low and peered through the heavy underbrush and bracken that sheltered him. A branch cracked again under the tread of a heavy foot, and Colin suddenly had a glimpse of armor glinting through the trees. He caught his breath and called in a low voice to the King, "They're coming, my lord!"

Bruce nodded grimly and reached into the quiver that hung over his shoulder. He pulled out an arrow and strung his great bow with it. Then he stood watchful and ready. He did not have long to wait. Three men, heavily armed, wearing coats of chain mail, came through the woods to the edge of the clearing. They halted almost beside Colin, who lay concealed, his hand buried in the deep fur of Bàn's neck. The men were obviously taken aback by their quarry's warlike stance, for they stood stock-still, uncertain of what to do next. They had meant to take the King by surprise, but found themselves confronted by an armed man, ready for a fight. Before they could alter their plan of attack, the Bruce called out, "Step forward, sirs, and give an account of yourselves! What brings you here, armed in such wise? You seem ready to do battle with a mighty army, yet I know of no such host

abiding in these parts that might warrant your attire."

The eldest of the men walked out into the glen and said, "Softly, cousin, softly. My sons and I have heard of your cause and are come to aid you in your fight. Put up your bow and give us leave to join you."

Bruce eyed the man mockingly and answered, "News travels slow, it seems. Where were you at Methven, cousin, or again at Dalry, when I had sore need of you? Nay, I think it passing strange that you should of a sudden throw in your lot with mine. Stand off, my lord," he added

sharply, as the man took a pace towards him. "I have naught to offer you in my service."

"You speak harshly, cousin," said the knight, advancing another step, "and by your manner you show that you have small trust in your own blood. Surely you are too hard on me. At least do me the courtesy of hearing my story."

Behind him, his sons moved out into the glen.

"I'll hear no more," Bruce replied in anger. "Words mean little, but deeds speak marvelous fair. It is enough that—" he broke off suddenly and raised his bow. "Stand back, I tell you, cousin, if you value your life. I'll not warn you again."

At that instant, the traitor drew his great sword from its scabbard and rushed upon the King. Swifter than lightning, Bruce loosed the arrow. It found its target, and the knight fell without a sound. With a cry of rage one of the sons sprang forward, wielding his battle-ax. But he had reckoned without Colin. Almost without thinking, the boy jumped from his hiding place and threw himself against the man just as he was about to hurl his ax at the King. The impact

of the boy's body made him stumble, and the weapon missed its mark. Bruce, who had drawn his short sword, reached him in one bound and put the blade through his heart. But the remaining son was attacking now. He was armed with a spear and, because of its length, he had the advantage over his opponent.

Colin, who was picking himself up from the ground where he had fallen, saw Bàn come charging across the grass. The man made a sudden lunge with his spear at the Bruce, but Bàn arrived at the same moment and leaped in front of his master only to receive the thrust full in the chest. Colin watched in horror as the assailant drew his spear from the dog's limp body and faced the King once more. But Bruce was upon him before he had time to ready himself. One blow from his sword shattered the spear, and he drove his point home. His adversary staggered a moment and then slumped to the ground, a few yards from his father's body.

Silence fell on the glen. Bruce leaned heavily on his sword and passed his arm across his eyes. Then, with a sigh, he let the weapon fall and knelt beside Bàn, lifting the dog's head in his arms. Colin crept forward now, his face wet with tears, and joined the King.

"Bàn, Bàn," the King said softly. "Most faithful and true of companions. How can I part from thee? But part we must, I fear, for thy wound is indeed a mortal one and beyond my power to heal."

The dog's liquid eyes searched his master's face, and his tail thumped feebly on the grass.

"Yes," said Bruce, "I know what thou would'st tell me. Life is a fragile plaything, fleeting and fraught with pain, and to lay down one's life for a friend is joy in part. But this I tell thee, Bàn: thou hast given thy life for mine. Although I take thy gift with sorrow, yet will I use it well. Hear me now and know that thy name will not be forgotten. One day, perhaps, all Scotland may have cause to thank Bàn, son of Righ, companion of Robert Bruce, for the gift he gave this day."

Colin looked at the dog, and as he watched, a shiver shook Bàn's frame. He gave a long sigh, and suddenly he seemed smaller in the protective circle of the King's arms.

Bruce laid him down gently and said, "Farewell, old friend. God speed you on your journey."

He stood up wearily and looked at Colin, who had turned his face away to hide his tears. Then he put his hand quietly on the boy's shoulder and said, "Come, lad, we must be off and away if we mean to reach camp by nightfall. See, the shadows are lengthening already. Lay aside your grief now, for grief is a sorry companion in an hour of need. Turn your face ever forward, Colin, for 'tis the road ahead your feet must follow. There is no turning back. Take memories with you, if you will, but ones to gladden the heart. This has been a sad day's work, to be sure, yet will I remember only the good in it — a boy who loved his King and came to save him and a dog who lay down his life for his master's."

So saying, he picked up his sword and bow and turned from the glen to the path that ran beside the burn. Colin followed him slowly.

The path was a rough one, and Colin was sore put to it to keep up with the long strides of the King. Bruce, noting this, slowed his pace until they walked side by side through the brake.

60

After a few minutes Colin asked timidly, "May I carry your bow for you, my lord?"

"Aye, you may carry it and welcome," returned the King with a smile, "if it will not tire you over much. You seem a frail lad for one raised in the Highlands. How is that?"

"I have been ill, sire, for a few months. But I am strong enough now," said Colin, and he shouldered Bruce's great bow proudly. "I was a baby to cry, I know," he added shamefacedly. "But you see I lost my own dog, Lad, in almost the same way that you lost Bàn today. I was in danger, and he pushed me out of harm's way, but he was killed in doing it. I was hurt a bit, some broken bones and the like, but my real hurt was losing Lad. Bàn was so much like Lad, sire, that when he died it almost seemed that I had lost my dog twice."

"Tears are not always a sign of weakness, Colin," said Bruce gently. "Else many a brave and valiant man would be branded coward. To lose what we love dearly is hard indeed. Such loss gives far more pain than the deepest wound made by sword or arrow."

61

Colin nodded gratefully, and they pushed forward in silence for a while. The sun had fallen now. Darkness settled over the rough countryside, and the air was chill. Suddenly the King touched Colin's arm.

"Look!" he said. "Yonder are the watch fires. 'Tis but a short way now to food and warmth and good cheer."

Colin looked ahead and saw the red glow of fires between the trees. But before he could answer the King, a figure slipped from the shadows and stood on the path before them. A sword flashed in the dim light, and a man's voice said harshly, "Halt, and give the password!"

"Free Scotland!" replied Bruce swiftly.

The man hastened to them.

"Thank God you're back safe, Robert. We have been well nigh in despair for fear that harm had come to you. My Lord Douglas and some of his men are searching for you even now. What kept you so long? Are you hurt?"

"Nay, Edward," said Bruce, "I am back safe and sound, thanks to this lad I have brought with me. His name is Colin MacNeill, and he has this day rendered great service to his King. But let us go back to the camp now. The day has been a hard one, and we both have need of rest and merry company. My tale shall wait until Lord Douglas has returned, since I would not tell it twice."

He threw his arm about the man's shoulders and said to Colin, "This is my brother, Colin. Had I a hundred more such true hearts to champion my cause, Scotland would soon be free. But, come. Fire and food await us."

They quickly made their way into the camp. When they reached the first of the fires, Edward Bruce said, "Go, my lord, and rest yourself till

Douglas's return. I will care for the boy and see that he lacks nothing."

The King smiled and said, "I leave you in good hands, Colin. But I will talk with you later this evening, for there is something that I wish to lay in your charge." He turned from them, and his tall form was lost in the shadows beyond the fire.

Colin looked at his companion curiously. Edward Bruce seemed younger than his brother. He had a merry face and was well built like the King, although shorter. He smiled at the boy and said, "And what will be your pleasure, Colin? Would you like to see our camp?"

"Oh, yes, please," said Colin.

And so Edward Bruce led Colin through the camp, introducing him to many of the men who sat by the fires eating and drinking. At length he brought the boy to a rough tent that stood near the largest fire. "Go in and rest for a bit, lad," he said. "For I have no doubt that the King will want your company at dinner."

Colin lifted the flap of the tent and started to enter it. There was a scuffling noise inside, and a

half-grown puppy appeared at the entrance. He wagged his tail at Colin and then ran out of the tent, his nose to the ground, apparently in search of something.

The King's brother laughed and said to Colin, "He's off to see his father." Then he suddenly looked puzzled. "Now that I think of it, I did not see Bàn with you when you came. That's strange indeed."

Colin looked at the ground and said in a small strained voice, "Bàn's dead, my lord."

"Dead!" cried Edward. "Alas, that's sorry news. A sad blow to Robert it must have been, for he loved the dog dearly. How did it happen?"

But before Colin could answer, there was a sound of hooves, and a band of horsemen rode into the clearing. At its head was a dark, strongly

built knight, who reined in his horse impatiently as he searched the camp with his keen eyes.

"Hola, Douglas!" cried Edward, and the newcomer turned his mount and rode over to them.

"Has he come yet?" he asked urgently.

"Yes, about an hour ago," said Edward. "He's in his tent and wishes to see you."

"Praise God," said Douglas with a sigh of relief. He leaped from his horse and handed the reins to a man standing nearby. "Take care of the beast," he said. "He's had a hard ride." And he walked swiftly off in the direction of the King's tent.

"I must leave you now, Colin," said Edward. "But I will call you when you're wanted, so be ready." He clapped his hand on Colin's shoulder and turned to follow Douglas's retreating figure.

Colin watched them for a minute and then entered the tent. He saw a pallet in one corner, and he went over to it and sat down.

"You've put in quite a day's work, Mr. Mac-Neill," said a voice beside him.

Colin jumped and then laughed. "You startled

me, Parsifal," he said. "Have you been with me the whole time?"

"Of course," said the Poddley in an injured tone. "You'd hardly expect me to leave you in the Highlands of Scotland, would you?"

"I guess not," said Colin. "And I'm awfully glad you're here. Parsifal, do you think the Bruce loved Bàn as much as I loved Lad?"

"Yes, sir, I do," answered the Poddley. "In a different way, perhaps, but just as much."

"Then, when Lad died I really behaved terribly, didn't I?" said Colin thoughtfully. "I didn't quite realize how terribly until now."

"Well, Mr. MacNeill," said Parsifal, "I think you're being very hard on yourself when you compare yourself with the King. After all, he's a grown man, and an unusual one at that, while you are still a boy."

"I know," said Colin, "but—"

Just then he heard a whimper from outside the tent. He got up and opened the flap, and the puppy that he had seen earlier pushed inside. He looked up at Colin, and his eyes were dark and sad.

"Why, it's almost as if he knew what had happened," said Colin wonderingly.

"Perhaps he does," said Parsifal. "Dogs are very remarkable animals, Mr. MacNeill."

"Come here, pup," said Colin, kneeling down and stretching out his hand to the dog. "Come on, boy. I won't hurt you."

The puppy crept over to him and snuggled against him with a sigh. Then he lifted his head and licked Colin's face.

"Hey," said Colin, laughing. "Don't do that! If my face needs washing, I'll wash it myself."

"He's rather appealing, isn't he?" said Parsifal. "I wonder what his name is."

"If he were mine, I'd call him Bàn after his father," said Colin, fondling the puppy's ears.

"That would be a hard name to live up to," murmured Parsifal.

"Oh, he could do it, I'm sure he could," said Colin. "Couldn't you, boy?" he asked the puppy.

The puppy just wagged his tail in answer.

The tent flap suddenly opened, and Edward Bruce came in. "The King asks your company at dinner, Colin," he said. He saw the puppy and added with a smile, "I see you've found a friend. You may bring him with you if you like."

So Colin and the King's brother went out into the firelight. The puppy followed at Colin's heels.

The King was seated by the largest fire, and at his right was Lord Douglas. When he saw Colin, he smiled and beckoned to him. Colin approached shyly and knelt before him.

"Sit down beside me, Colin," said Bruce, "and share our meal with us. This is the boy I spoke of," he added, turning to Douglas. "A brave lad and a true one. I am in his debt."

Douglas leaned forward and laid his hand on Colin's shoulder. "We are all in your debt," he said, his dark eyes resting on Colin's face. "Men will long remember the day that a boy and a dog saved Scotland."

Colin blushed fiercely and looked down at the ground. He could think of nothing to say and was groping desperately in his mind for some fitting rejoinder to this tribute when the puppy crept forward and lay down beside him. The King laughed. "It seems you have a way with dogs, Colin," he said. "I see that now is the time to speak of what I would give you in remembrance of this day. Nay, lad, wait—" he added as Colin started to protest. "I know what you would say—'Loyalty demands no payment.' But a gift given for friendship's sake is another matter entirely. And this is what I would give, Colin MacNeill—a token of my friendship. Surely you cannot deny me that?"

Colin looked wonderingly at Bruce and answered softly, "No, sire."

Bruce smiled. "Then, Colin," he said, "in the name of friendship, I give you something of great worth to me—and to you, I think—something young, as you are, something full of trust and of promise, as you are. I give you Bàn's son. May he serve you long and honestly, as his sire served me."

Colin gave a small gasp and looked down at the puppy beside him. The dog looked back at his new master and wagged his tail.

"Thank you, my lord," the boy said falteringly, his eyes dimmed for a minute with tears he didn't quite understand. "I love him very much and will take good care of him always."

73

Bruce looked quietly at Colin's happy face and said, "I know that, Colin, or else I could not have parted with him."

"Have you named him yet?" Edward Bruce asked Colin.

"Not really," said Colin. "I know what I would like to name him, though."

"And what's that?" asked Douglas, a smile lighting his dark face.

"Bàn," said Colin. "After his father. It's a name to live up to, I know, but I think he can do it."

"'Bàn' it is then," said the King. "And now, my lords," he added, rising to his feet, "I ask you to drink with me to young Bàn and to the MacNeill, his master. May fortune smile on them!"

He grasped a flagon and raised it to his lips. Douglas and Edward Bruce did likewise. "Bàn and MacNeill!" they cried.

Colin had never felt so proud. He straightened his tired back and looked at the men around him. The firelight flickered on their faces and seemed to burn their likenesses into his mind—Edward

Bruce, young and impetuous, his handsome features lit by a gay smile; Douglas, homely and dark, a bold strong face with great wit and courage in it. But clearest of all was the face of the King whom Colin had grown to love so well. As he looked, Colin fancied he saw in it all the qualities of greatness — honor, wisdom, faith and, above all, a warmth and compassion. It seemed a face that would inspire men to deeds of valor beyond their ordinary imaginings. Colin stood silent and motionless as if in a dream, but suddenly he felt a sharp tug at his sleeve. He regretfully turned his attention to Parsifal, who was whispering urgently, "It's almost time to leave, Mr. MacNeill. Please start thinking about nothing right away!"

"Oh, couldn't we stay a little longer?" begged Colin. "Please, Parsifal."

"Gracious, no," replied the Poddley. "If we miss this time wave we'll be in all sorts of trouble."

"All right," said Colin regretfully, and he closed his eyes and started to think about nothing. Suddenly, however, he opened them again.

"Parsifal," he said, "you forgot about Bàn!"

He looked for the puppy but couldn't see him anywhere. He was just about to run off in search of the dog, when Parsifal quickly said, "Please, Mr. MacNeill, do as I tell you. Concentrate on nothing immediately. I have the whole situation well in hand."

So Colin did as he was told and presently found himself back in his hospital room, dressed once more in his striped pajamas. He looked at the clock on the wall and was astonished to see that only one hour had passed since his departure. "Why, that couldn't be right," he said aloud.

"Oh yes," said Parsifal, appearing beside him. "It's quite right. Time waves are wonderfully convenient. I don't know how I'd manage without them."

"What about Bàn?" asked Colin anxiously. "You haven't forgotten about him or lost him somewhere between there and here have you?"

Parsifal drew himself up to his full height of twelve inches and frowned at Colin. "Mr. Mac-Neill," he said in a very reproachful tone, "I will

77

put down your seeming lack of confidence to fatigue brought on by your adventures in the Highlands. I have neither forgotten Bàn nor lost him. You will simply have to show a little more patience. I am not a magician, you know, only a Poddley, and I have to do things my own way."

"Oh, Parsifal, I am sorry," said Colin ruefully. "I didn't mean to sound ungrateful and doubting. It was just that I promised the Bruce to take good care of Bàn, and I got a little worried. Please forgive me."

Parsifal smiled and said quickly, "Never mind, sir, don't give it another thought. Now perhaps you had better get a good night's sleep, for you have a big day ahead of you tomorrow."

"Okay," said Colin, climbing into bed. "And Parsifal," he added, as he pulled up the covers, "thank you for everything. I'll never forget my adventure as long as I live. It was the most exciting thing that has ever happened to me."

"You're welcome," said the Poddley. "I enjoyed it myself. And what's more, I was very proud of you, Mr. MacNeill. You were breaking bread with some very great men tonight, but you

79

held your own in their company. Now then, sir, good night and pleasant dreams. Tomorrow is another day."

And Colin, who had opened his mouth to speak, yawned instead, and fell asleep immediately, a smile on his lips.

Parsifal settled himself in the chair beside the bed and disappeared. It was time to call in to Control Center, and he was rather looking forward to it.

After reporting the doings of the day, he asked, "Any special instructions?"

"First of all," said Control Center, "congratulations on a job well done. You have shown imagination and inventiveness, and I take pleasure in informing you that you are being nominated for Poddley of the Year honors."

"Good gracious!" exclaimed Parsifal.

"However," continued Control Center, "we feel it advisable to recall you for a forty-eight-hour pass before you take your next case. You have been on five assignments in a row now without a break, and no one does his best work when he is tired. Therefore you must report in to headquarters no later than nine o'clock tomorrow morning."

"But Mr. MacNeill doesn't go home until nine," objected Parsifal. "I did want to see him safely home and settled comfortably. And what about Bàn?"

"I'm sorry, P654321, but those are your orders," said Control Center. "I'm sure you can explain things to Mr. MacNeill. You've given him your word about the dog, and he trusts you. He shouldn't be too upset. Nine o'clock sharp, remember. *Over and out.*"

Parsifal sighed. He felt his star growing cold and knew that there was no use arguing with Control Center. He would just have to find a way to explain things to Colin. The night seemed very long.

Morning came at last, however. Colin awoke full of excitement. "Will I see Bàn today, Parsifal?" he asked.

"Yes, sir, you will," said the Poddley. "But, Mr. MacNeill, I will not be with you when you do. I have received orders to report in by nine o'clock this morning, so I must leave you."

"Oh, Parsifal!" cried Colin, his eyes filling with tears. "I can't go home without you. Don't go, please don't go!"

"I have to," said Parsifal simply. "As you grow older, sir, you will find that there are things that have to be done whether one wants to do them or not. Besides, my job here is finished. You are well now, and you are going home to your mother and father, who love you very much. Whether you realize it or not, it's better this way. Life is made up of endings and beginnings. Your illness has ended, and you are going to begin your normal way of life again. Your need for me was when you were ill, and if I have done my job satisfactorily, you should not need me any more."

"But I'll miss you so!" faltered Colin.

Just then there was the rattle of trays in the hall, and Parsifal said, "I haven't much time, sir, so listen closely and don't interrupt. They'll be in with your breakfast in a moment, and then I'll have to go. Don't worry about Bàn. Trust me. I won't let you down. Always remember that learning is a source of great joy — one that will

82

never fail you. And if you ever want to send me
a message, just think it to me—I'll get it."

There was a brisk rap on the door.

"Good-by, Mr. MacNeill," said Parsifal. "Eat
a good breakfast." And suddenly he was gone.

Colin ate his breakfast dutifully enough, but his heart wasn't in it. He was dressed and ready to go when his parents came. They were so happy that he tried to seem happy too, not to disappoint them. He said good-by to all the doctors and nurses who had taken care of him at the hospital and then went with his mother and father to the car.

The ride home was a silent one. His mother turned to him once and said, "You're awfully quiet, darling. Do you feel all right?"

"Oh yes," said Colin. "It's just that I'm thinking."

At last the car pulled up before his house, and Colin opened the door and got out. He stood looking up at the house, and his parents watched him eagerly. On the front porch lay a half-grown puppy. It looked at Colin and then got up and started down the steps towards him. Colin's mouth dropped open, and his face turned pink. "Bàn!" he cried in a voice filled with joy. The puppy's tail wagged furiously as the boy ran to meet him. They greeted each other like long-lost brothers, and Mr. MacNeill remarked to his wife

with a smile, "It's almost as if they had met before somehow."

And far away in time and space, a Poddley received a message. "Thank you, Parsifal! Thank you so very much for everything!"

The End